Bloom

SNEHA NARAYANAN

PRAISE FOR BLOOM FOR YOURSELF

Sneha Narayanan explores the relevant themes of body positivity, self-love and self -acceptance. Using exquisite wordplay and delicious metaphors, she portrays her heartfelt thoughts with elan.
- Pankaj Giri, Bestselling Author

A truly fascinating journey of a powerful woman. She transforms every moment of her existence into a response worth writing down. What a startling, beautiful book! Definitely a Rupi Kaur in making.
- Anu Lal, Author

Pristine writing by author Sneha Narayanan. Reading this book is like submerging deep into the labyrinth of emotions and finding a new meaning to self-love and self-acceptance.
- Swati Khatri, Author

Such a beautiful compilation of poems. I cannot believe she is a first-time author! The writing is top-notch, she weaves her words like magic.
- Inzamamul Hoque, Amazon Reviewer

Brimming with emotions after reading these beautiful poems. Exceptional!
- Upasana Singh, Amazon Reviewer

Gave me Goosebumps! All the poems have a lot of depth. This book teaches you to be kind, to think positive and to love yourself.
- Vaishali Jain, Amazon Reviewer

A beautiful amalgamation of inspiration and courage, these self-help poems are based on self-acceptance. Empowering and thought-provoking!
Priyanka Godse, Amazon Reviewer

One of the best books that I have read on Self- acceptance. Completely blown away!
- Swati Sharma, Blogger

Miss Sneha Narayanan has eminently jotted down strong human emotions in a very subtle yet striking manner.
- Catherine Gudiwada, Goodreads Reviewer

SNEHA NARAYANAN

Kalamos Literary Services LLP

Kalamos Literary Services LLP
Email: info@kalamos.co.in | editorial@kalamos.co.in
Published in 2021
by
Kalamos Literary Services
ISBN- 978-93-90909-37-7

Typeset in Kalamos Literary Services LLP

Cover designed by Brand Inspire OPC Pvt. Ltd.
Print and bound in India.

For you, **Daddy and Mommy**
I love you to the moon and back

For my amazing **Readers,**
I am nothing without you.

PART – 1
BODY POSITIVITY AND
SELF ACCEPTANCE

AM I NOT BEAUTIFUL?

They say,
too thin, too fat,
too curvy, too flat.

Growing up, they said,
Beauty is fair skin,
flaunting almond eyes,
glossy black straight hair,
a shapely feminine nose
that suggests both regality and softness,
and an hourglass figure
representative of
my reproductive abilities.

But I am not fair-skinned.
My thighs jiggle.
My tummy protrudes a little.
My eyes are too tiny
and nose too broad.
My cheeks - reminiscent of
the baby fat I carried
all through high school, and
my untamed curly hair -
the cherry on top.

I clearly do not live up
to the cardboard version of

feminine allure that can stop men
in their tracks.
So, am I not beautiful?

A DIALOGUE WITH SELF

There is this voice inside of me,
that pierces my calm
in hushed whispers,
ricocheting against the walls
of my heart,
and serves to me lazy insults
in a drawl
the suavest conman would envy:
My biggest critic.

Sometimes when I exchange dialogues
with my inner voice,
my self-confidence reduces to rubble.
My self-esteem chafes against the floor.

I look in the mirror
and I don't like what I see.
The voice says, "You're ugly!"
"You're not good enough."
"Is that all you can do?"

But, not good enough for whom?
Why do I engage in critical self-talk?
Why do I let my doing-ness
obliterate my being-ness?

I need to be kinder to myself,

detangle my perspective
from needless comparison with others
who do not live in my body
and know not the battles
it has fought
and conquered.

AM I CURVY?

"No, way! You are beautiful",
they say.

Though my face has a smile,
secretly I wonder, *why can't I be both?*

Being thin doesn't equal being beautiful,
And being curvy doesn't make you ugly.

Oh, how beauty standards operate
in binaries!
And the measure of humans
weighed upon these vagaries.

Maybe, the mirror does reflect lies,
Till as long as you don't awaken to your truth.

I awoke to the kaleidoscopic
shades existing inside of me, making up
my mind, body and soul.

I was more than
just a 'Yes' or 'No.'

MORE THAN A ROSE

It is when
I look at the rose, freely blooming
in her soft-lipped, wine-red glory,
not once caring about the thorns
that try to dim her shine,
or the sinful fingers that pluck it
without mercy,
that I realize
its magnificence
lies *in its acceptance*
of simply being
the miracle
God made it to be –
Be it in the thick of the woods
or between the pages of
your favourite book.

Happiness is a choice,
not materially or physically bound.
Remove the blindfold,
look around.

LOVE ME FOR WHO I AM

You are skinny! **Eat something**.
You are piling on weight, **start dieting**.

Your words steal the glitter
from my eyes,
while my morale resembles
a shrivelled poinsettia.

However flawed I might be
In your gaze,
Can I not be loved and wanted
for who I am?

I don't expect melodies
to slide off your lips,
but maybe,
a little kindness could soothe
old burns,
inflicted by an air-brushed world
not attuned to my realness.

FACING THE MIRROR

Your exposition on my body is gross,
For I am not born to be
your five-course meal,
served hot and grandiose.

Your intrusion on my body is not accepted,
As body shaming is simply ill-bred.
Who gave you the sanction to
mock my imperfections?
Boxed and stereotyped,
I am more than your trivial tea-time discussion.
Who gave you the right to hurt my sentiments?
All I can see now is a once-poised girl
tucked into the folds of resentment.

I don't want to deprive myself of food,
Is dieting *any* good?
I want to drape myself in
the finest lace,
and not have to worry about
hiding my generous waist.

'Tis true, I am tired of trying to please others.
But perhaps, I will first need to face
my own skin in the mirror.

A NOTE TO MYSELF

I will not wait
for your heart to bloom
to a shade you may never have seen;
I will soak myself
in unconditional love
for the way I've always been.

My body, my choice.
And I shall not let
anyone tell me otherwise.

MY FOREVER LOVE

"But nobody would
want a girl like me,
I'm not pretty enough." She whispered.
"Only pretty girls get boyfriends."

I wanted to reassure her,
that her Prince Charming was out there,
waiting for her somewhere.

And then I walked back to the teen me:
Wanting to be loved, waiting to be cherished
with open arms,
to be told there was no one quite like me.

But I was, perhaps, still a caterpillar.
And, no boy ever looked at me.

Now no longer the invisible, withered wallflower
from back in my days of naivete,
I soon compared it
to life in my twenties;
When I was the heartthrob of every man ---
A world in oases of empty, broken, covetous hearts.
Pursued like a flaming desire and
treated like a queen.

What changed? I wondered.

Except that I'd lost twenty kilos,
and had started applying make-up.
Rising up to the notion of femininity,
some would say.

Is love so superficial? I questioned
my sonorous depths.

Having someone love you,
doesn't automatically increase your worth; but also,
just because someone doesn't love you,
does not reduce your worth to rubble.

Between those arduous days
and nights of waiting for the perfect love
to sweep me off my feet,
and the days of glory where the sun
wouldn't turn from my face,
I harked back to a firestorm
throbbing in my ribs,
a peace washing over the scars
inflicted by a cruel society,
that yes, I was already perfect.
Whole. And cherished.
I just couldn't see it yet.

That is when it dawned on me,
that I'd never needed a knight in shining armour

to save me,
Because I *was*
my own saviour, my eternal lover.

PRETTY THINGS

So, I whispered to her,
Pretty things don't need loving.
They are pretty because they're already loved.
And guess what?
The fiercest of this love springs
from the well of your own being,
that is unscathed by fleeting opinions
of this temporal world.

Dare to look within.
You might just find the only one
who can save you.

THE SUN SHINES ON ME TOO

Fair and lovely?
That's not me.
Peachy silky skin
with apple-tinted cheeks?
That's not me either.

I am more
acne scars,
body hair,
with some extra flab here and there,
garnished with a smile
that can bulldoze
over your prejudice.

Stop scorning my being,
just because I don't fit
into your perception of beauty.

Everybody is beautiful.
There's space in this world
for a rose, an orchid,
a sunflower, a cactus.
Just don't pluck it,
with your tainted fingers.

FAT SHAMING

Do not judge me by the scars on my face,
I am a lot more than the flab around my waist.
Even at my thinnest, I have always felt fat,
Some would say, "Girl, why don't you lose some weight?"

Because of people like you, I ended up with low self-
esteem.
So, stop giving me the side-eye when you see
me relishing my ice-cream!
Instead of punishing myself trying to
look slimmer,
I chose to fall in love with myself
Till the noise around me grew dimmer.

Fat shaming is offensive,
Stop ridiculing.
Because it is nothing
But a sign of bullying.

UN-APOLOGY: YOUR NEW BEGINNING

Stop apologising for your supposed imperfections,
nobody's perfect.
Stop scarring your own flesh
with barbed wires
of unworthiness, 'not-enough-ness' and shame —
making an enemy
of the unique gift that you are.

Why do you need validation?
Why do you feel the need to *belong*?
To something? Or someone?
Rather than yourself, first and foremost?

What can the riches pour into you
that you do not already own?
What can lack and poverty steal from you
when your spirit is overflowing
with the sheen of your light,
and you make no attempt
to disguise it,
for the fear that you will be left
with dark corners
to hug …

And how can the mirror dictate
your fate,
before you get a chance to

embellish it with your fire and calm?

Think about it
before you crinkle your eyes at
the only being who will
stand by you, come rain or shine.

WHAT DOES MY SATURN SAY

You feel content
when you score remarkably
in the game of life,
earning brownie points doggedly.

But,
do you feel mistaken
when you seek contentment in external pleasures,
and feel regret licking
at the pit of your stomach?

I feel flawed
when I see myself stuck in this vicious pattern,
using social validation
and my carefully curated beauty as a crutch
to appease and shush
my inner Saturn.

The more I try to bury the echoes
of self-flagellation,
the louder it boomerangs in my ears.

CUE EXIT: THE VALIDATION GAME

Bombarded with compliments and attention,
and pampered to the fullest,
we find our worthiness
for a fleeting moment in time,
in joys springing
not from our own ribs.

It's like binging chocolates,
the upturn of a see-saw;
We get a brief high.

But why do we need validation?
Why do we look for supply
and fix?
Why do we measure our worth
based on others' opinions about us?

There is always going to be someone,
more beautiful,
more successful,
thinner, smarter or richer.
The grass is always going to look
greener on the other side.

But when will we get the chance
to soak up the sun on our own backs
and tend to the shade on our own porch

if we're constantly looking
for the moon and the stars
on the other side of the fence?

WHAT BEAUTY REALLY IS

Beauty is a reflection of your soul,
Compassion and depth
make it whole.
Beauty is not necessarily when you look your best.
It is, *when you give your best.*
Pour your innocence into the living
and the inanimate around you.
Like it's your first and last shot at life.
Like you're coursing through
that next big adventure,
but also have a morsel to eternity
to spend watching the sunsets and the butterflies.

You may not look like a million bucks,
But you are empathetic and kind hearted,
You come alive with a force of your own
That no fire or storm has ever shown.
Unfortunately, it does not hold much value
in today's superficial world,
that is used to filters
than real skin and bones.

Your success and physical appearance may fade,
But your inner beauty will continue to
enthral , charm and invade,
the hearts of those who speak
the same language as yours.

For it has a unique character;
more than its presence, its absence is felt.

IT IS OKAY IF YOU ARE DIFFERENT

It is okay whether you are fat or thin,
Why try to fit in?
It is okay if you are not tall,
We are different after all.

Does it make a difference if you are dark or fair?
No one does really care.
Why try to follow the crowd?
It is fine to be different, say that aloud.
Here is a fun fact and it is true,
It is really okay, to be you!

ON REPEAT

Through mangled looks of
judgment, cracked mirrors
and even a stray pimple or two,
Tell yourself that,
You are beautiful,
You are happy,
You are kind,
and worthy of love.

Repeat this to yourself,
till it reverberates
in your core.
Stop putting yourself down.
Stop hiding.
Stop trying to please others.
Put those walls up
where you need to.
Learn to say No
and mean it.

Let your presence speak for you.

PART – 2
POSITIVE THOUGHTS
AND HAPPINESS

THE MIND TREE

Our thoughts are like seeds,
From these seeds, emerges the tree.
Each thought and feeling,
is our creation.
A conversation with the Universe…

For the tree to be strong, the
seed needs to be sown
and watered right,
and allowed to bask in the right amount of sunshine,
while kissing blissfully
the hope and aroma of the first rains
of the season.

From this robust seed
arise thoughts that bloom in the wind,
weaving strong and beautiful relationships,
as much with oneself
as with others.

So choose wisely:
*What do you wish to plant
in the fertile ground of your mind?*

HAPPINESS IS A UNIVERSE INSIDE OF YOU

Today if someone talks to you nicely,
You get elated and impressed.
Tomorrow if they are nasty,
You get hurt and depressed.

But why is
your response dependent
on others' behaviour?

Our happiness or pain,
cannot depend upon others,
our jubilation and exuberance
cannot be tied to their whims and fancies.

It is only
when our core reverberates
with the realisation of the earth, the sun,
the moon, the oceans and the skies within us
can we truly be separate from,
and still one with all.

Only then
can we embrace
our wholeness.

ALL YOU NEED IS YOU

Pull yourself away
from negativity.
Surround yourself
with loving, positive thoughts.

Let the little things be,
allow bigger joys and bigger doors
to greet you.

And while you ride
the tides of life,
love yourself like you would
that lover who left you at the
downtown bridge
saying he'd come and whisk you away
from this sordid world
but never did.
And you waited anyway.
Hoping where even hope
would hang its head in shame.

For all you need is you.
And you.
And you.

NIRVANA POINT

Do you think,
happiness depends upon
you achieving some laurel or fame?

That the sun will somehow
shine brighter on your face
if you succeed
in devouring
those daunting goals?

Wake up and look around,
before you run out of breath
measuring the distance
between your wobbly legs
and your wraith-like pale form
at the supposed Nirvana point.

Failure and success,
are not in our hands
but our thoughts and feelings are.
Let hope and faith be
your guiding light where
sweat and blood alone
cannot surmount
those intangible walls in your path.

AN EVERYDAY THING

We are pebbles of divine design
thrown into the all-knowing, resolute
waters of fate.

We don't always fall
to our depths in the same way.
We don't always
cause ripples
loud enough
to disrupt
the order of the universe.

Some of us turn pale,
the poison of life's vicissitudes
working against the crimson blush
of our cheeks.
While others among us
coast along the journey
of being human
and fallible.

The heat and the thunderstorm
and the chill of the wintry grey skies
will cease to be.
Those who have hurt us
will fade away from the imprints
of our memories, someday,

and we will accept
the absence of wanting and pining
and turning over our
aching sides in bed
and flicking the light switch
on and off
and just settle for a cup of tea
in the balcony
like it's an everyday thing.

The control of our thoughts is
in our own hands;
Awareness of the same and
choosing to then see rainbows is the key.

What do we see,
when we look up at the skies?
That is all that matters.

THE ANATOMY OF HAPPINESS

Happiness can arrive despite
the obstacles on our path.
It is in how we respond on the inside
to the stimuli,
before we can touch it on the outside
and give it worldly labels,
for our much-limited human comprehension.

Happiness is rarely ever,
only a destination.
It is but a river deep within our soul
that snakes its way
between mountains, valleys, and
sleepy towns etched in stolen memories -
soft yet undeterred,
before it can kiss the sea
in its own time.

Happiness is the fruit of
tranquillity and
oneness,
reconciled between the mind, body, and spirit,
come rain or shine, praise or wrath,
should we have the courage to
truly seek it.
First and foremost —
in ourselves.

SALVATION ON A FERRIS WHEEL

Happiness is a Ferris wheel:
You have to know how to enjoy
the adrenaline of your peaks,
when it is your time,
so, you can partake in the
bliss of others soaking in
their rise
in their time.

You are not a clown;
So why do you need to go out
of your way to amuse others?

Instead, you can do wonders
and spread the light off your shine
by being jovial, by being
true to *yourself*.

We try to make
others happy because,
We think that if they are happy,
We will be happy too.

But,
You cannot make others happy,
by doing something for them,
at the expense of your soul,

by always being the giver,
the constant fixer-upper.

If you wish to see others around
you happy, and empowered,
fill your cups up to the brim,
 so, they know no other way
than to spill over the edge,
right into their minds and hearts.

Salvation resides on your tongue;
when you dare to taste it fully,
you lead others to do the same.

BUILDING RIGHT…BRICK BY BRICK

Relationship exceeds
the boundaries of definition,
Be it between a parent and his child or
a man and his wife.

Relationship is an exchange of energy between souls,
love makes it whole.

Love is the basis of every relationship,
and our thoughts are the foundation
of our relationships.

Hence, you need to check your thoughts,
so that the foundation is pure
and nourishes the world created between
you and those you love.

Focus on the foundation,
Only then the building of your interactions
will be taken care of.

POSITIVE THOUGHTS

Today is the result of our past,
So think before you blast
Tomorrow will depend upon our today,
Invest well so that it repays
Positive thinking has the power to make our life better,
Strive well and let's have a prosperous future

Your thoughts are created by you,
Your reactions are always your choice,
Positivity will deliver its due,
While negativity will just create noise
Our thoughts make our fate,
So think positive and have faith

Let us not wallow in criticisms and negativity,
It leads to suffering infinity
Do not spread an ocean of misery,
Appreciate others success and victories.

THE MONSTER IN MY MIND

When a thought is created,

It leaves an impact fated.

The heart follows as mandated,

Emotions are then generated.

Based on those feelings,

Behavioural pattern changes.

Between bleeding and healing,

This mortal outrage ranges.

I wish I could lock away

My tremulous mind, for once.

And let not these monsters sway

My bliss of a thousand defiant suns.

SECRET TO HAPPINESS

It is not possible to be cheerful
all the time,
Feeling blue is not a crime
More than circumstances or situation,
It's your negative thoughts that cause frustration.
It is natural to feel unhappy
when things don't go your way,
That does not mean it is a bad day

A happy life does not mean
having all cheerful moments,
Life is not always filled with
happy components
When your mind is at peace,
And your worries cease,
The contentment you feel is happiness.

BE KIND

Compassion goes a long way,
It gives mental peace and
keeps your anger at bay
Kindness is that seed,
Which when sown results in good deeds

Spread love and humanity,
Hatred is insanity
When was the last time that you were kind to someone?
Nothing as rewarding as a kind act done
Everywhere you go,
Let some kindness flow.

HOW TO TREAT OTHERS

How would you like to be treated?
With love and respect, and not mistreated
Treat others how you want to be treated,
Speak how you would like to be spoken to
If you wish ill towards someone,
Aren't you wishing ill towards yourself too?

As long as you have wisdom,
Happiness and peace remains,
As long as you deliver kindness,
Friendship and love awaits.

NEVER GIVE UP

Remind yourself that it is okay to fail,
Successful people also sometimes trail
Don't feel so let down,
We all have our ups and downs
Do not give into your fear,
For every struggle is worth its blood and tears
Pick yourself up and look forward,
Do not believe anyone who says you are a coward
It is going to be okay someday,
Put your worries at bay
Never stop and keep trying,
What you think is the end,
May be is just the beginning

IN DEFENSE OF BEING AVERAGE

Being average is abhorred and detested
But, is being mediocre something bad?
Why are we conditioned to prove we are the best?
If every person becomes someone extra ordinary,
Then no one will remain ordinary!
What matters is not how to avoid failing,
Rather learning how to get up after you fall.

So, learn from every mistake you make,
instead of getting upset and crying,
Making mistakes imply that you are trying.
Why being average isn't debated?
Mediocrity, I feel is highly underrated.

STOP BLAMING OTHERS

You might feel angry or frustrated,
For a person or situation that was anyways over-rated
They annoy you, you say,
Within minutes, they would spoil your day
If only they would listen to you,
You feel your troubles would be few

Well, it's your life-boat,
Take control of the rudders,
It makes you powerless,
When you start blaming others

You will get weak in tough times,
You will get bleak in rough times,
But you will be fine, just recline on a chair
They will try and shake you,
They will try and break you,
But you wouldn't fall if your conscience is there

You may be rich, you may be pretty,
But these attractions are merely ephemeral,
Take command of the slaves,
running all through your mind,
Because your heart is eternal

BLAME GAMES

Castles fall.
The orchids wither.
Laughter fades away
in the grind of time, and life,
that spare none.
And that is where
fingers are pointed,
scapegoats are birthed,
victim cards used aplenty.
For how else
can a human being
accept the uncertainty
and imperfection
of living through the
good, bad and ugly?

Blame games erupt,
depleting vital life force
in the process.

Unbeknownst to our egoist selves,
We lose years of our lives
in this entrapment,
while getting mentally exhausted.

Would it not be prudent instead
to take responsibility

for our own actions
and our state of mind
than blame what exists
outside of us?

ART OF ADAPTING

Sometimes we need to change with circumstances,
Life becomes easier to survive
Sometimes we need to take risk,
It has its own reward in abundance

Whenever one feels cowed down,
Under the pressures of life,
Then adapting is the best tool,
To convert impossible to possible

It is not the sunny times but adversities
That makes us clear about our priorities,
Indulgence takes a backseat,
And minimalism takes the hotseat.

GRATITUDE

Be thankful for today,
Be grateful for every birthday
Be thankful for mornings with its light,
Be grateful for the dark and night
Be thankful for the sun that shines,
Thank god for every dime

Be grateful to every heart that gave you joy,
Be grateful for the beating of your heart,
When things don't go your way,
stop grumbling,
Life is not always about complaining

We often take our lives for granted,
Forgetting the hands that gave us shelter and blanket
Show gratitude towards your parents,
Their love for you is so apparent
Life is a beautiful thing,
Count your blessings.

PART - 3
CAGED BIRD – THE AWAKENING

VIRTUE AND VICE

You can't prohibit me
from wearing what I want,
Nor can you force me to wear something
I don't want to.

My clothes do not define
my personality or character.

Because let's be honest -
You're associating character
with false, patriarchy-imposed modesty.

Isn't it time we realize
that modesty is personal
and a choice to be exercised
in individuality?

Let us not equate it
with the moral high-ground of virtue.

THE UNFORGIVEN

Labels look good
on product packages
and women who dare
to fall in love too soon,
or so, say the men
who call us 'easy', 'whores',
'sluts', All the while marking themselves
As cool studs!

We are made to feel guilty,
for things we do and don't do,
for being and not being.
Broken relationships? Chalk it up to us!
Too loud, too soft-spoken?
Too aggressive, or a push-over?
Got married too early? Don't want to marry ever?
The noise never leaves us,
even as our souls catch dust.

Truth be told – we are guilty for just existing.
Being a woman
In this man's world.

And so, they will not forgive us:
For voicing our opinion,
For wanting our freedom,
For being unapologetic,

For snatching what was rightfully
ours in the first place-
The right to choose.

WHAT FEMINISM IS NOT

When will this world understand?
That feminism is neither nudity, nor modesty,
Nor is it about opposing men
For the sake of it.

It is simply about having a choice,
A choice to do what you want to
without the fear of being judged,
penalized outside
the hallways of justice on 'moral grounds'.
Or worse, killed.

STOP OBJECTIFYING

The length of our dress
is no measure of our consent.
Why then, do you men,
Shame us so, causing torment?

Sexism underlines your irrational demands;
You say you're only
trying to protect us,
but wish we'd instead be slaves
to your command.

Why teach *us* to wear "decent clothes"?
Objectification is your middle name.
So maybe,
you deserve to be loathed.
What we wear on our skin
gives you no right to assault.
Oh, you know it too well
it isn't the damsel's fault!

THE DEVIL'S SUPPER

The victim is blamed and shamed,
Bystanders let the depravity spill,
calling it her fate;
5 months or 50 years,
it's all meat and bones
served on the devil's plate.
They call it rape,
But she's the one
enduring the hate.

TOMORROW IS A NEW DAY

Another day knocks at my door.
I look forward filled with expectations.

Will today be the one to fill the void
deep inside of me?
Will today be the moment I'll finally
be able
to climb out of the treacherous pit
called life, and the chaos it wields?

My tears have dried up,
my cheeks feel like crumbled
autumn leaves.
A sigh escapes my dazed lips,
as I throw a reminiscent glance
at the road I have travelled so far,
and feel the weight of the hurdles
I've crossed along the way ---
the pain and anguish
hammering at my soul, every single day.

"It is a new day," I tell myself;
armoured with fortitude - my sole companion.
Up there, perhaps,
a new God too
who will not turn away from me

and heed my harrowed cries
for the darkness to end.

ACKNOWLEDGEMENTS

I have suffered from low self-esteem and body image issues for as long as I can remember (this goes back to my school days when I recall being mostly overweight and friendless). Not surprisingly, I never had a healthy relationship with food. I either count calories and overly restrict my food intake or binge on whatever I can lay my hands on.

No matter how conflicting my relationship with self was, I still craved to be accepted, make friends, be chosen as part of a circle, and be loved for who I was. I thought most of the problems in my life would vanish automatically, if I could lose weight and "look beautiful". Never once realising, that the answer lay within me – in **self-acceptance** – and beauty, truly is, in the eyes of the beholder.

A part of me has always sought approval and yearned to belong - to "fit in" and to be showered with admiration. I was always searching for love and validation in others, but my ability to love myself was almost non-existent. And that's when I realised if I cannot love myself, how can I expect others to love me?

I have penned this book from the bottom of my heart and if you, my dear reader, find yourself in the pages of this book, all I want to say is:

Please be kind, to yourself as much as you are to others. Be grateful for the body and soul you are – because trust me, there's no one quite like you. Think positive, and love yourself fiercely. It doesn't matter whether you are fat or thin, dusky or fair, tall or short. You are *you*, and nobody can take that away from You.

Bloom. And *Bloom For Yourself.*

Coming to the few steadfast people who've seen me through this journey:

First and foremost, I would like to thank my parents, Lt. General Narayanan and Gayatri Narayanan, for their unconditional love, support and guidance at every step - be it in life or through the phases of doubt I felt while writing this book. Mom, Dad, I derive my strength, perseverance and compassion from you. Also, a big shoutout to my baby brother, Kartik Narayanan, for his invaluable contribution -   not just in making this book happen but for also being the light of my life. Much before I'd dreamt of making my words count.

I am immensely grateful to my friend and editor, Shravani P.T. for editing my poems so beautifully. She is extremely talented, hardworking, and absolutely in love with her job – which shows – in how she took my labour of love and turned it into something magical. She's not just a thorough taskmaster; she has an incredible heart too - a total delight for all authors. Shravani, you are the wind beneath my wings and I cannot thank you enough.

Next, I would like to thank my friend, Nishant - a writer, therapist and a restauranteur. Nishant, this book wouldn't have been possible without you encouraging me to give poetry writing a shot, even if I had never done it before. Thank you for your time, patience and unconditional support throughout this journey. Thank you for standing by my side through it all.

I would also like to thank Ishan Agrawal and his team, a literary agent and book reviewer, for helping with my book's marketing. Thank you, Ishan, for playing a pivotal role in making my kindle version of the book an Amazon bestseller for many weeks after its release.

Last but not the least, I am immensely grateful to my publishing team at Kalamos Literary Services. I can't thank you guys enough for giving me this opportunity to make my thoughts heard.